A YOUNG PERSON'S GUIDE TO

New Orleans Houses

L. VOGT 9

A YOUNG PERSON'S GUIDE TO

New Orleans Houses

BY LLOYD VOGT

PELICAN PUBLISHING COMPANY

Gretna 1992

Library of Congress Cataloging-in-Publication Data

Vogt, Lloyd.
    A young person's guide to New Orleans houses / by Lloyd
Vogt.
        p. cm.
    Summary: Surveys the varying styles of houses found in
New Orleans and how they evolved.
    ISBN 0-88289-829-9
    1. Architecture, Domestic — Louisiana — New Orleans —
Juvenile literature. 2. New Orleans (La.) — Buildings,
structures, etc. — Juvenile literature. [1. Architecture,
Domestic — Louisiana — New Orleans. 2. New Orleans (La.) —
Buildings, structures, etc.]
I. Title.
NA7238.N5V65 1991
728'.09763'35 — dc20   91-15213
                                                            CIP
                                                             AC

Manufactured in the United States of America

Published by Pelican Publishing Company, Inc.
1101 Monroe Street, Gretna, Louisiana 70053

INTRODUCTION

The city of New Orleans is one of America's greatest "outdoor museums." The thousands of houses that line its streets are examples of types and styles of architecture from all over the world, including unique houses that originated right here in New Orleans.

To understand New Orleans houses is to begin to understand New Orleans, because the buildings in a place tell us a lot about the people who built them — about their history, their values, their ingenuity, and what they considered beautiful. Like New Orleans itself, the houses of the city come from a number of cultures — French, Spanish, African, and, later, American — and many other nationalities. Their hopes, dreams, and ways of life are expressed in the buildings they left behind.

Most of the great houses of New Orleans were built before there was air-conditioning. The distinctive personalities of much of the architecture of the city were created by the clever attempts of different people at different times to deal with the sub-tropical climate of New Orleans. They built houses raised above the damp ground to provide good ventilation; high ceilings let the heat rise off of the floor, helping to keep the rooms cooler in the summer. Large porches provided a covered outdoor space to sit, and sheltered doors and windows so they could stay open during summer rains, letting the cool, moist air blow through the house. To keep themselves warm in the winter, they built numerous fireplaces — sometimes one for each room!

In order to understand New Orleans houses, you have to understand two main concepts: **type** and **style**. The house **type** is a matter of its shape and the arrangement of its rooms. **Style** is determined by the ornament (*see glossary for this and other terms in heavy, dark print*) and trim on the house, and by things such as its windows and doors.

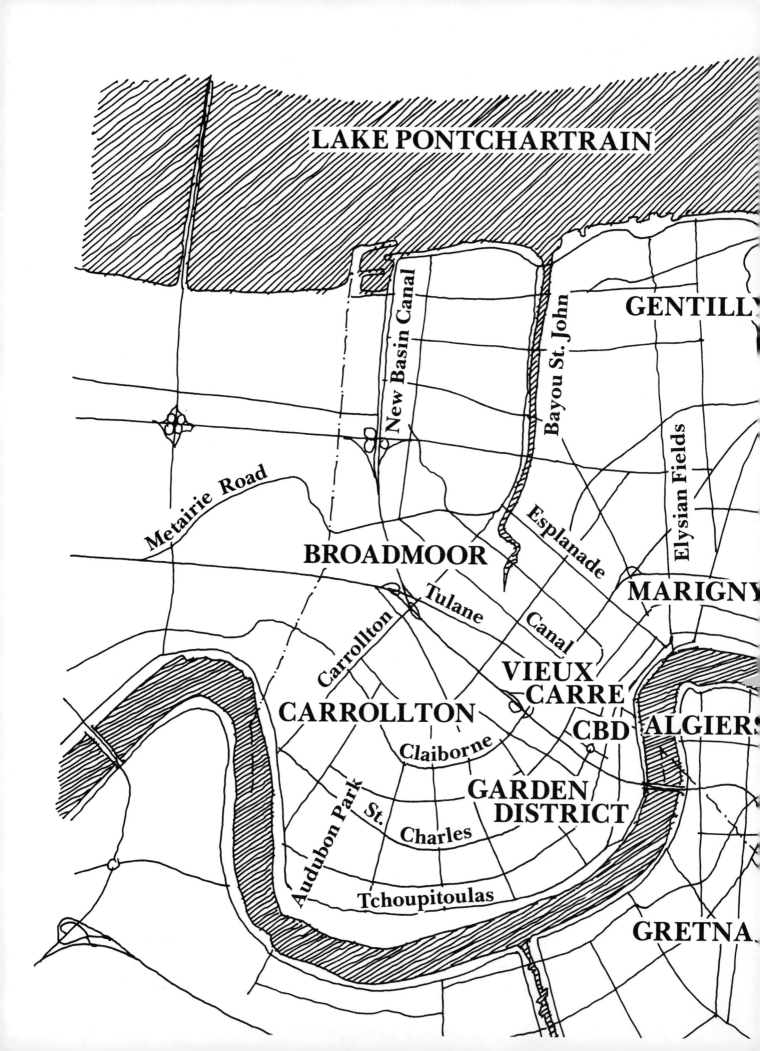

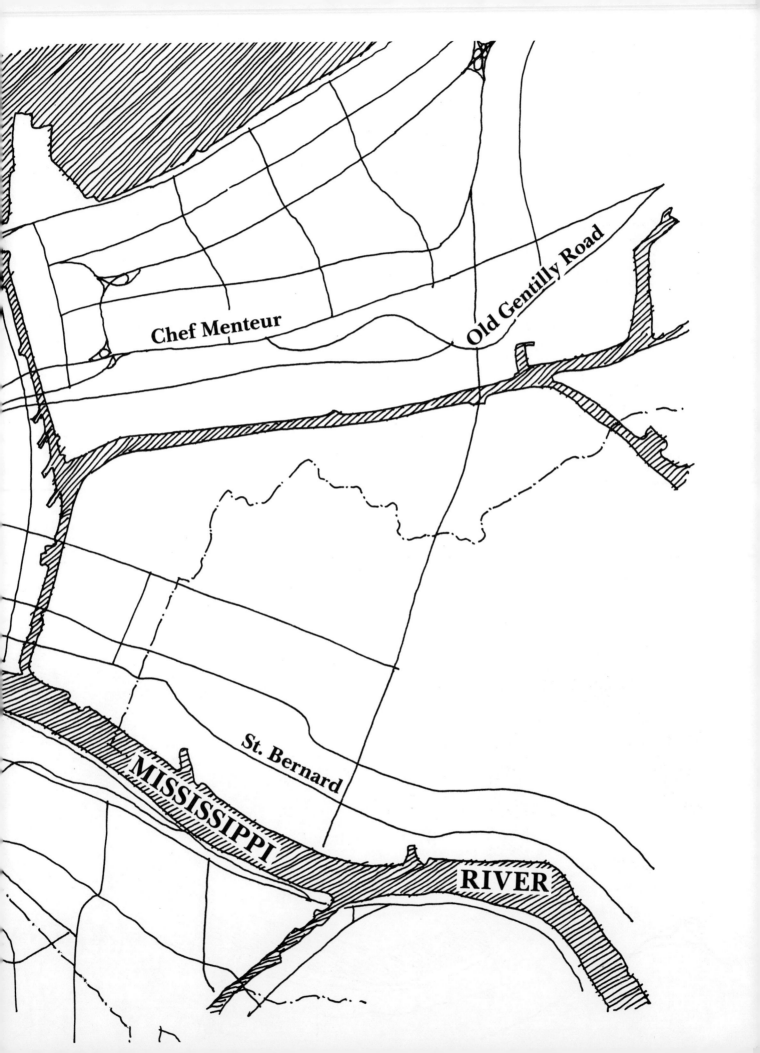

HOUSE TYPES

Some of the most common house types found in New Orleans are pictured on the following pages. These house **types** were often built in several **styles** during the various periods of the city's history. In the following section, we will look at some of those styles and what makes them different from one another.

FRENCH COLONIAL PLANTATION HOUSE

These houses were built from the early 1700s to the early 1800s. They were shaped like a rectangle or a square and usually had two stories, with the main living area on the second floor. The first floor was generally used for storage. On the second floor was a large, open, covered area called a **gallery**. It was on one or more sides, sometimes running all the way around the second floor of the house. These houses had either **double-pitched** or **hipped roofs**, and frequently had **dormers**. There are not many French Colonial houses remaining in New Orleans, but they are very important because they represent one of the most significant periods in the history of the city: its beginnings as a colony of France.

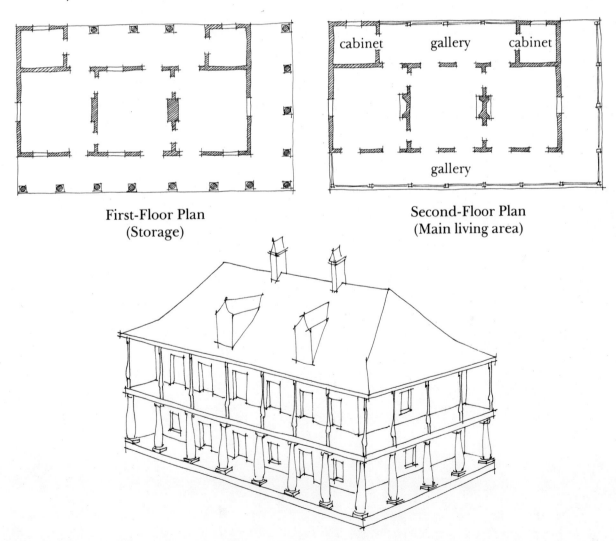

First-Floor Plan
(Storage)

Second-Floor Plan
(Main living area)

CREOLE COTTAGE

Creole cottages were popular from about 1790 to 1850. They were the most common house type found in New Orleans during the early 1800s. They are generally rectangular, and most were built very low to the ground and right up to the sidewalk. They had four rooms, two fireplaces, and two small rooms on the rear called *cabinets*. The earlier cottages had hipped roofs, while the later and most common ones had a **side-gable roof**. The Creole cottages built outside of the city in the rural areas were raised a few feet off of the ground and had a front porch with wooden columns.

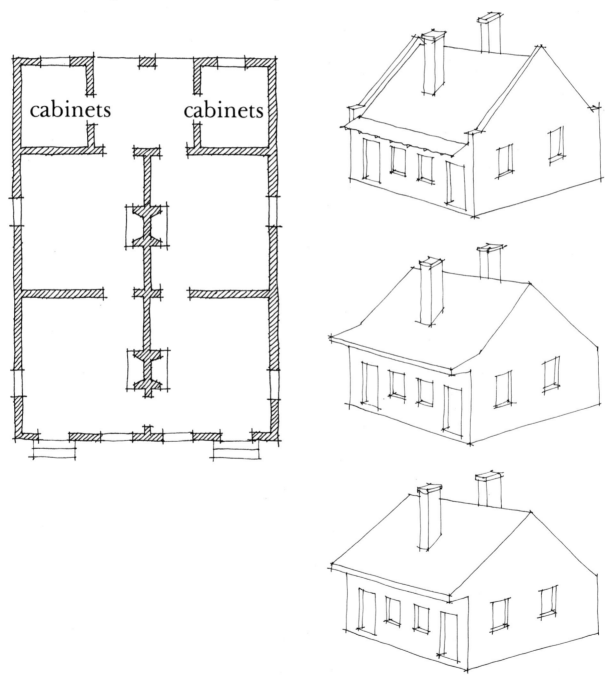

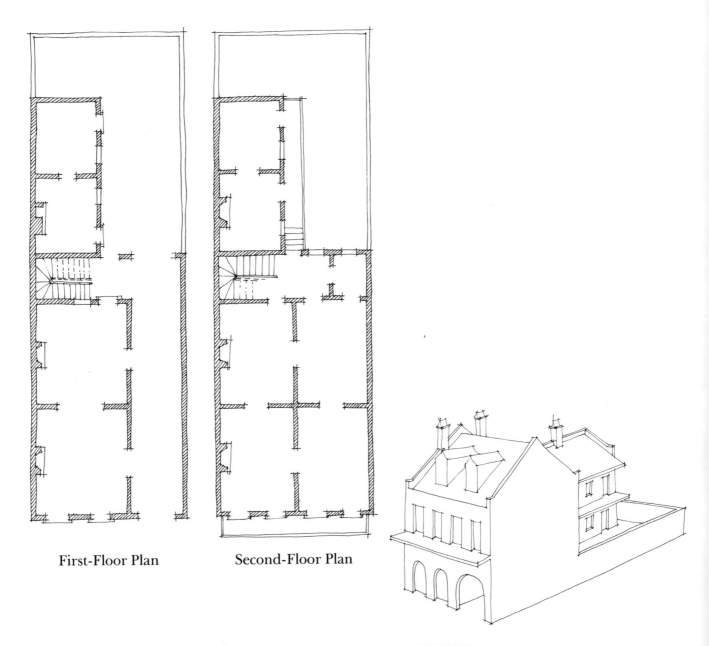

First-Floor Plan   Second-Floor Plan

PORTE COCHERE TOWNHOUSE

This building type, whose name means "coach door" in English, was common in the French Quarter from about 1800 to 1850. These two-, three-, and four-story buildings had a carriageway entrance leading to a **courtyard** in the rear where the carriages were parked. The carriageway was generally **arched** and located on one side of the front of the house. The ground floor had two rooms which were often used as a shop, while the upper floors were used as living quarters. A wing for the servants was attached to one side of the rear of the house, forming one wall of the rear courtyard.

Another type of townhouse had a passageway only large enough for a person and not a carriage. This type is called a Creole townhouse.

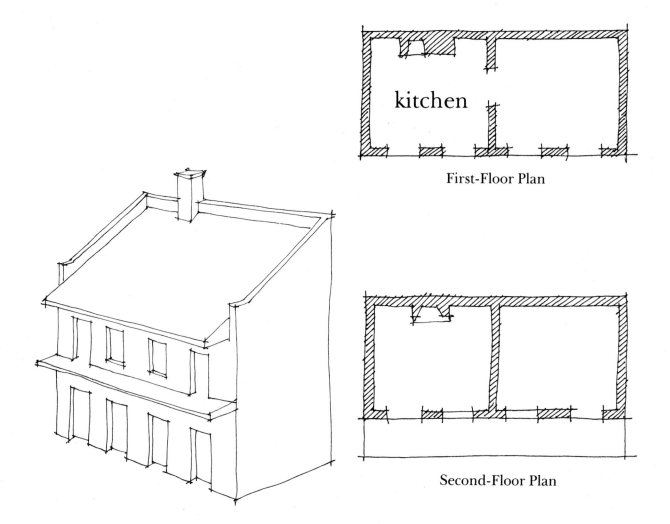

First-Floor Plan

Second-Floor Plan

OUTBUILDINGS

Outbuildings were support buildings for the main house. They were commonly associated with Creole cottages and townhouses from the early 1800s until about 1860. During the early part of the 1800s they were generally separate buildings in the rear yard of the main house. Later it became common to attach the outbuilding to the rear of the main building. Outbuildings varied from one to three stories in height, and contained a kitchen, a storage area, and sometimes a dining area on the first level. The kitchen was separated from the house because of the heat it generated and because of the threat of fire. The upper level(s) had bedrooms that were used by the servants and sometimes by the older boys of the family.

AMERICAN TOWNHOUSE

The American townhouse was introduced into New Orleans during the 1830s, and was a house type which was influenced by the townhouses being built in the northeastern United States at the time. It is similar to the Creole townhouse, but its entrance-ways are much fancier and are usually **classical** in style. While the passageways and stairways in the Creole townhouse are on the exterior of the building, the American townhouse has an interior hallway and interior stairs. Like the Creole townhouse, it generally has a wing for the servants attached on one side of the house in the rear.

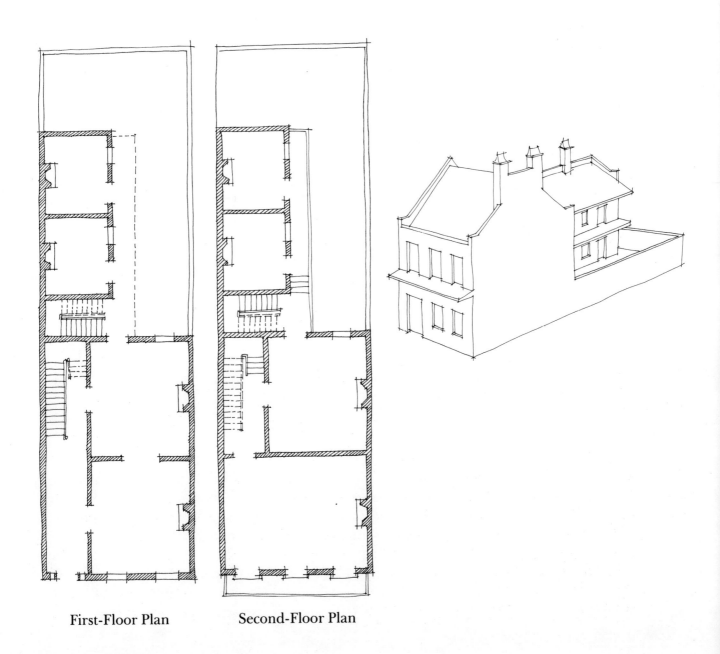

First-Floor Plan   Second-Floor Plan

AMERICAN COTTAGE

Inspired by the **Georgian**-style houses of New England and the Northeast, the American cottage was first introduced in New Orleans in the 1820s, and it remained popular until the 1870s. It has a five-**bay** front porch (five openings divided by columns), and a very detailed entranceway in the center. It has two rooms on each side of a center hall and two small rooms called *cabinets* in the rear, similar to the Creole cottage. Most American cottages have a steep side-gable roof with dormers.

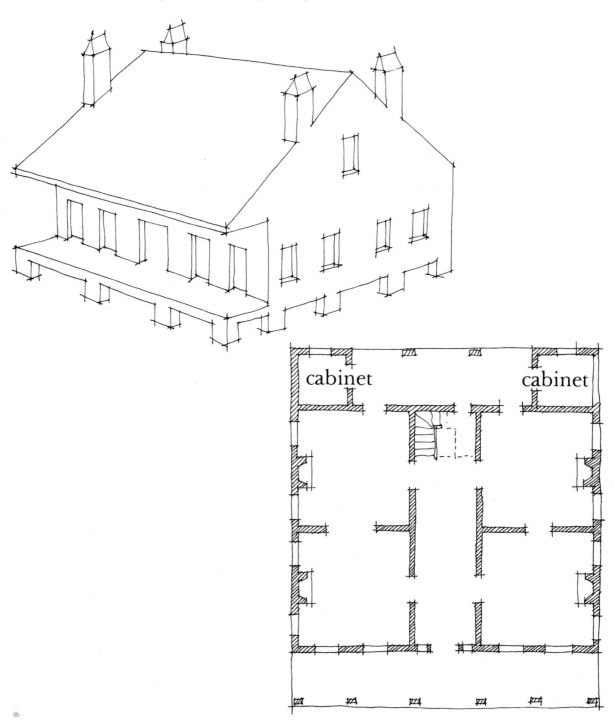

SHOTGUN SINGLE

The shotgun is a long, narrow, rectangular house with all the rooms arranged directly behind one another in a straight line, front to back. The term "shotgun" is said to have been created from the idea that if a shotgun were fired through the front door, all the pellets would leave through the rear door without hitting anything.

The shotgun house type is thought to have come to New Orleans in the early 1800s from the Caribbean island of Haiti, where it was created from the blending of African and Haitian Indian house types. Shotgun houses are very common in New Orleans. Their popularity continued until about 1940.

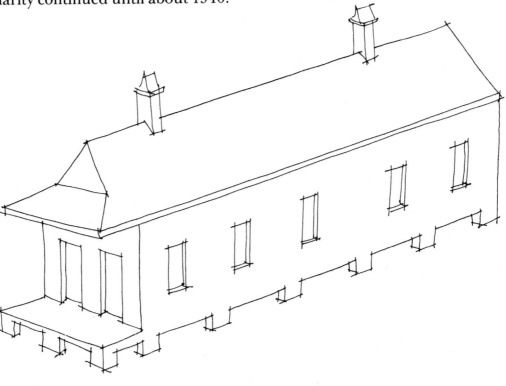

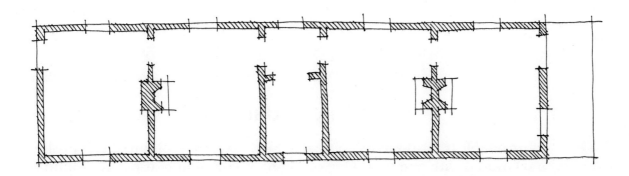

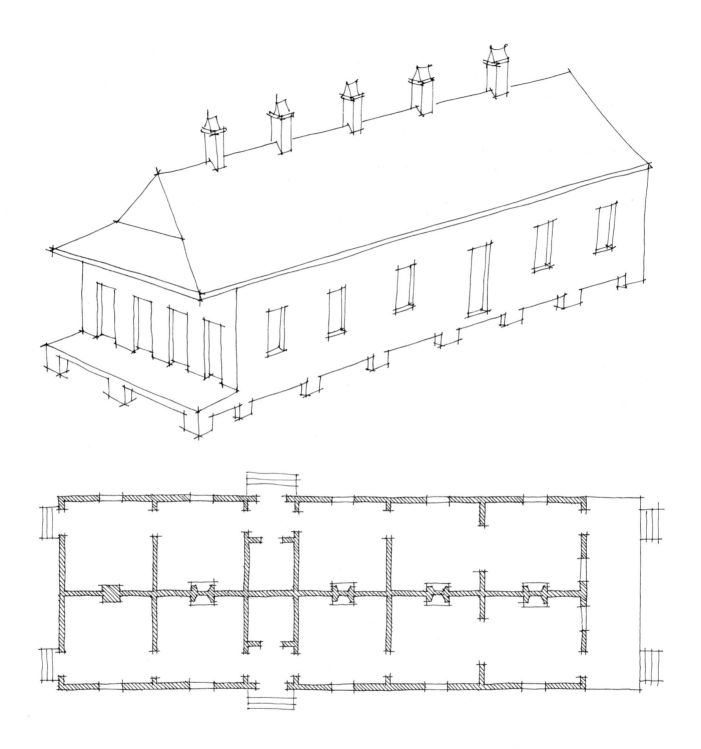

SHOTGUN DOUBLE

The shotgun double is a two-family house that looks like two shotgun singles pushed together and covered with one roof. One of the most common house types found in New Orleans, shotgun doubles were built from about 1840 until about 1940. Sometimes an owner will create openings in the center wall dividing the two sides and make a one-family house out of the double.

CAMELBACK

The camelback is a shotgun single or double which has one story in the front and a two-story section in the rear, much like the hump on a camel's back. This house type most likely developed in New Orleans. Camelbacks were common in New Orleans from the 1860s to the early 1900s.

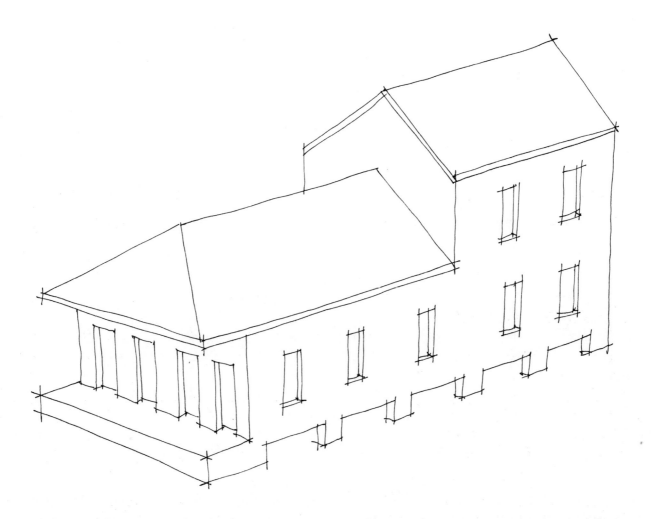

GEORGIAN COLONIAL

The Georgian house type is very symmetrical, orderly, and "formal" in its composition. That is, its two-story square or rectangular shape contains a floor plan that is balanced. The house is divided by a center hall with two rooms of the same size on each side of the hall. It has a hipped or side-gable roof. The Georgian Colonial style came to New Orleans as a "revival" of a style which was popular in the northeastern United States in the 1700s.

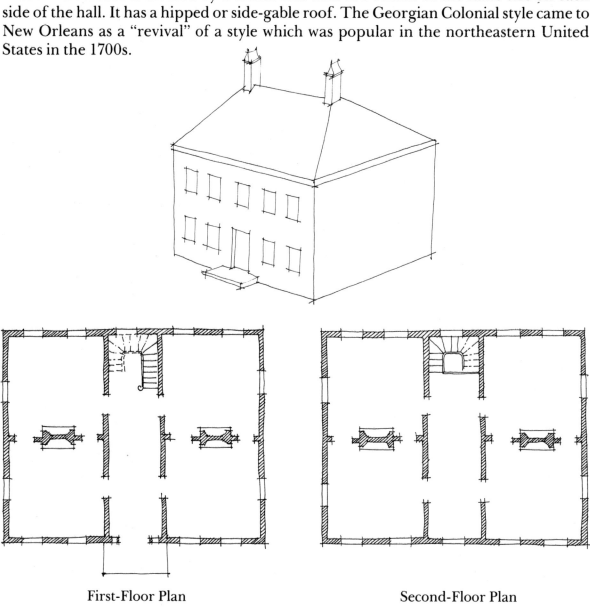

First-Floor Plan   Second-Floor Plan

The majority of the houses in New Orleans are one of these basic **types**. In most cases, when a house type was developed or introduced in the city, it was used over and over. In different historical periods, different **ornaments**, **trims**, windows, doors, and columns were used, creating new styles. The next sections discuss the major periods (or eras) of New Orleans' history, and look at the architectural styles that were developed in each one.

THE COLONIAL PERIOD (1718-1803)

In January of 1699 the French-Canadian explorer Pierre le Moyne, Sieur d'Iberville, and his younger brother Jean Baptiste, Sieur de Bienville, sailed into the Gulf of Mexico with four ships and about five hundred men. They were on a mission for Louis XIV, king of France. They landed on the Mississippi Gulf Coast near where Biloxi is today, met with the Indians who lived there, and formed a peace treaty. They established a settlement, built a small fort, and left eighty-one men to protect the settlement.

Some of the explorers continued westward, where they soon discovered the Mississippi River. They traveled northward up the mighty river about a hundred miles, where they met some Indians and explored the site where they would eventually build New Orleans. They left without trying to establish a settlement.

In 1718, Bienville returned to the site he had visited nearly twenty years earlier and founded the settlement he named *Nouvelle Orleans*, after one of the king's most powerful assistants, the Duke of Orleans. They laid out the streets where the French Quarter is today, and began building houses and other buildings.

The first houses built by the French settlers were temporary structures, and they soon rotted, cracked, and settled in the damp soil, or were destroyed by floods or hurricanes. More permanent buildings were soon introduced, but many still were not suitable for New Orleans. They were built very low to the damp ground, and so they rotted quickly. They did not have porches or good ventilation, so they were very hot and stuffy.

As Creoles (a word meaning anyone who was born in the New World to European parents) from the Caribbean islands began to move into New Orleans, they began to construct houses that were more suitable for the climate. Very experienced in dealing with the tropical climate of the islands, they introduced raised buildings, porches, and high ceilings.

In 1762, Louisiana came under the control of Spain through a treaty with France. During the period of Spanish rule that followed, many things happened which shaped the architecture of the area. There were two great fires, in 1788 and 1794, which destroyed most of the buildings in the French Quarter. The Spanish introduced strict rules for building, including fire-prevention features, to prevent this type of disaster from happening again. The French Quarter became much more urban, with two-and three-story attached brick buildings with courtyards replacing the original simple, one-story, wooden houses. The bricks were covered with plaster to protect them from moisture.

Although the Spanish controlled the government for almost forty years, Louisiana kept much of its French character, including the language, culture, and traditions. In 1800, France regained control of the area. Three years later, New Orleans was sold to the young United States as part of the Louisiana Purchase, bringing an end to the colonial period in New Orleans.

THE PITOT HOUSE

The Pitot House, on Bayou St. John, is a good example of a French Colonial plantation house. The main living area was on the second level, while the first floor was used for storage. The house was built in the late 1790s. One of its early owners was James Pitot, the first elected mayor of New Orleans.

DOUBLE-PITCHED ROOF

TURNED-WOOD COLONNETTE

VERTICAL-BOARD SHUTTER

WOODEN BALUSTRADE

GALLERY

STUCCO

FRENCH DOORS

DORIC COLUMN

L. VOGT 91

THE POSTCOLONIAL PERIOD (1803-1830)

Soon after the Louisiana Purchase, Americans began to move into New Orleans, a city which had developed a reputation as a place of opportunity for all classes of people.

The Creoles, separated from the Americans by nationality, religion, customs, and language, considered their culture superior to that of the newcomers; meanwhile, the Americans didn't trust anyone who did not speak English. Both groups were determined to keep their own identities, their cultural traditions, and their lifestyles.

Most houses built during the Postcolonial period were one-story Creole cottages and two-and three-story townhouses with their outbuildings. From 1820 to 1835, as more and more Americans moved into the city, there was a gradual shift from Creole to American building, with influences from house designs in the northeastern U.S. In the French Quarter and its surrounding neighborhoods, the buildings began to be built as row houses, which were identical buildings, sometimes as many as twelve, attached to one another. Houses of the late postcolonial period also began to use some classical (ancient Greek and Roman) details.

CREOLE COTTAGE

This Creole cottage looks like many found in and around the French Quarter. Like most, it has two doors and two windows on the front, and it is built very close to the sidewalk. It has a side-gable roof and two dormers.

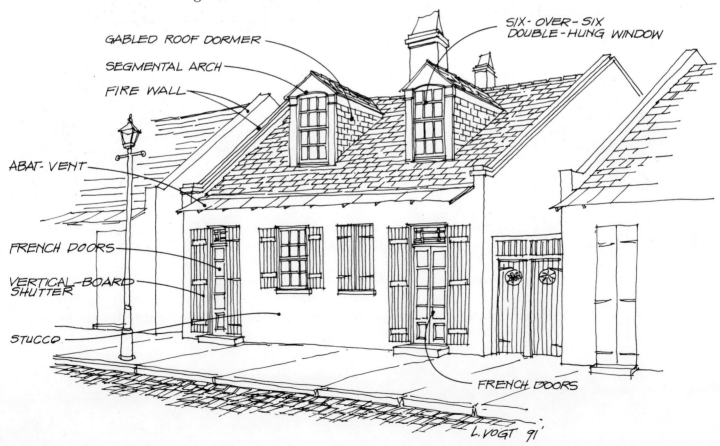

GABLED ROOF DORMER

SEGMENTAL ARCH

FIRE WALL

SIX-OVER-SIX DOUBLE-HUNG WINDOW

ABAT-VENT

FRENCH DOORS

VERTICAL-BOARD SHUTTER

STUCCO

FRENCH DOORS

L. VOGT 91'

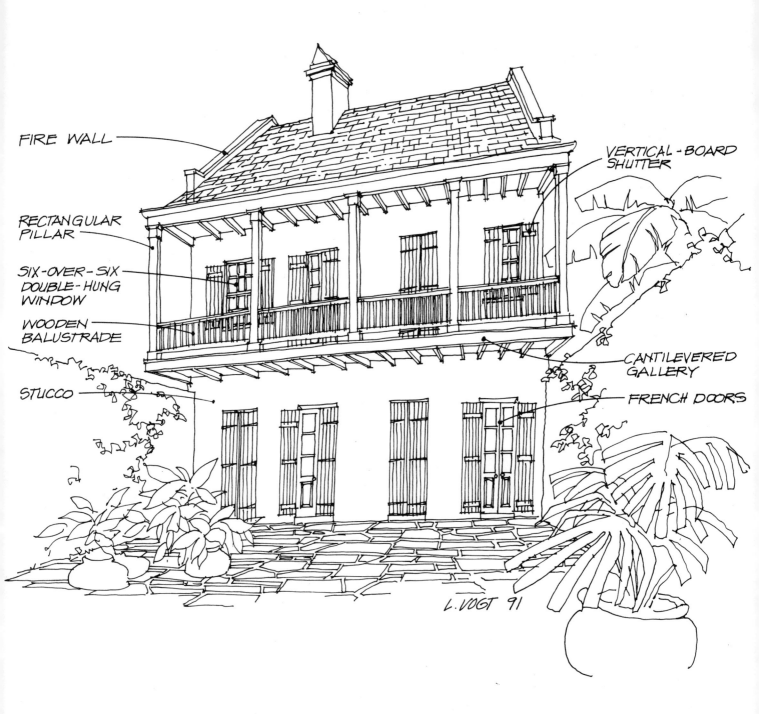

FIRE WALL

RECTANGULAR PILLAR

SIX-OVER-SIX DOUBLE-HUNG WINDOW

WOODEN BALUSTRADE

STUCCO

VERTICAL-BOARD SHUTTER

CANTILEVERED GALLERY

FRENCH DOORS

L. VOGT 91

OUTBUILDING

This outbuilding is located in the back yard of a Creole cottage, and forms one side of the courtyard. It is two stories high. The ground floor has a storage room and a kitchen, and the second floor has two small bedrooms for the servants or the older boys of the family.

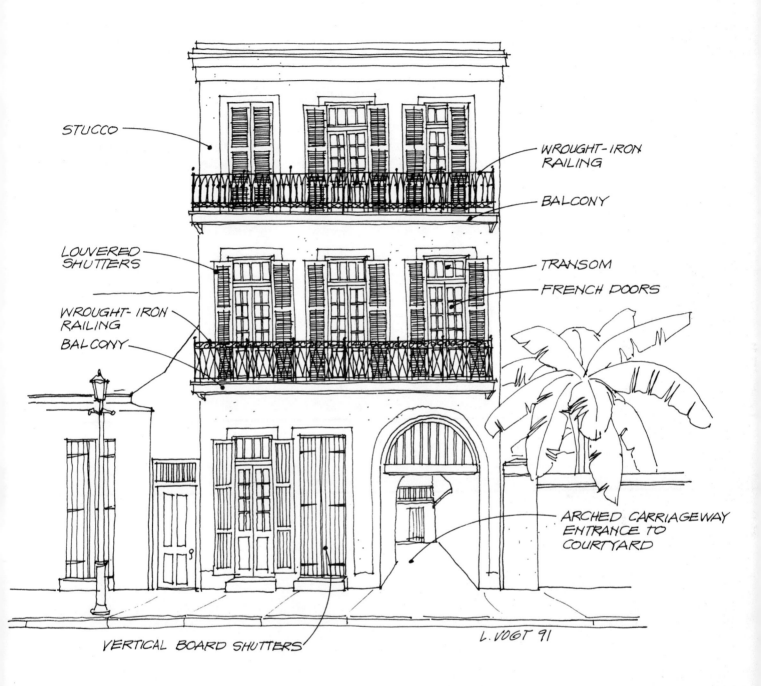

STUCCO

WROUGHT-IRON RAILING

BALCONY

LOUVERED SHUTTERS

TRANSOM

FRENCH DOORS

WROUGHT-IRON RAILING

BALCONY

ARCHED CARRIAGEWAY ENTRANCE TO COURTYARD

VERTICAL BOARD SHUTTERS

L. VOGT 91

PORTE-COCHERE TOWNHOUSE

This porte-cochere townhouse has a large, arched carriageway entrance on the front. The carriageway is paved with stones and leads into a courtyard in back. The courtyard is planted with banana trees and has a fountain in the middle. These courtyards are very common in the French Quarter, and the sight of them at the end of a long carriageway can offer us an exciting glimpse into the past.

THE ANTEBELLUM PERIOD (1830-1862)

The period between 1830 and 1862 was the most glamorous and the richest in the city's history. New Orleans was the home of many wealthy cotton and sugarcane planters. Fancy riverboats and tall sailing ships were docked along the riverfront. People from other parts of the world were arriving every day, and new buildings were being constructed all over the city. New Orleans had fine restaurants, grand hotels, an opera, and frequent celebrations, including balls, banquets, and parades.

New Orleans was the wealthiest city in the United States. The city was growing rapidly and by 1840, with more than 100,000 people, it was the third largest city in America.

The American townhouse, with its interior sidehall and stairway, became very popular. By 1830 even the Creoles were beginning to use the exposed red-brick designs of the Americans, and slate (a black or grey stone) was replacing clay tile and wooden shingles as the most common roofing material. Around this time, houses also began to feature classical Greek details, beginning the Greek Revival style that would dominate New Orleans architecture for the next thirty years.

There are three major **orders** of classical Greek architecture: the **Doric**, **Ionic**, and **Corinthian**. These orders were first used in the construction of temples in ancient Greece. In New Orleans, the most frequently used orders were the Doric and Ionic. The more detailed Corinthian order was not widely seen until the Italianate style became popular in the late 1850s.

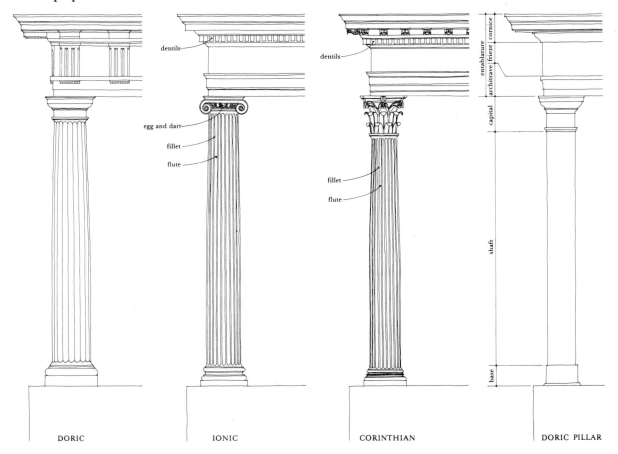

In New Orleans, the most popular house types of the antebellum period were five-bay American cottages, American townhouses, shotguns, camelbacks, and double-gallery houses, which had one gallery built over the other.

In 1861 the Civil War began, bringing an end to the antebellum (Latin for "before the war") period.

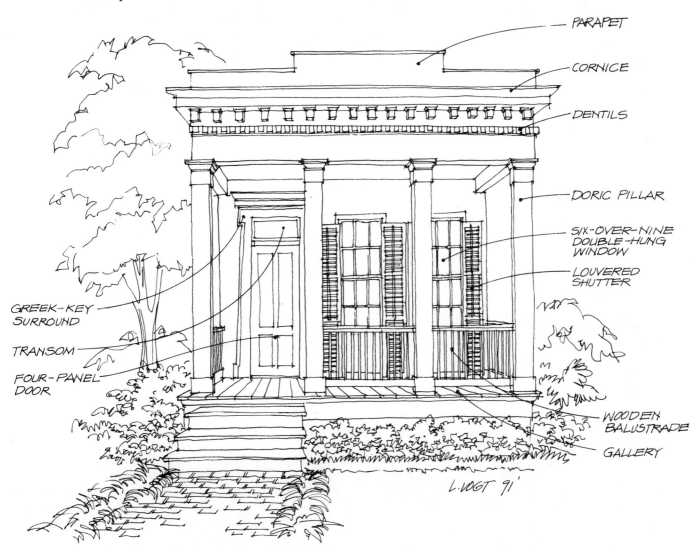

GREEK REVIVAL SHOTGUN HOUSE

Greek Revival houses are very common in New Orleans. They are very much influenced by the architecture of ancient Greece. Greek details were put on many different house types of this period. The house shown here is a shotgun single house. It has rectangular classical columns made of wood, which support an **entablature** with teethlike decorations known as **dentils** and a simple, undecorated **parapet**. The front door has four panels and a **transom** above, while the windows, with shutters, are full length (opening all the way down to the porch floor) and have six windowpanes over nine.

GREEK REVIVAL RAISED AMERICAN COTTAGE

Because the Mississippi River and heavy rains sometimes flooded New Orleans, many houses were raised high above the ground. This raised American cottage is in the Greek Revival style. It has a center hall and a large front door, with two windows on each side.

THE VICTORIAN PERIOD (1862-1900)

After years of copying the ancient Greeks during the antebellum period, Americans wanted to concentrate on the present and to develop a new style of their own. The houses built during the Victorian period were very different from the Greek Revival houses of the antebellum period. They were more complex, with many different kinds of exterior decorations, and in many colors.

The Victorians liked variety and playfulness and disliked classical detailing. Carpenters could easily find fancy woodwork, made in steam-powered sawmills and bought from catalogues, and they used this woodwork to decorate the Victorian houses in many different ways. The Italianate style developed during this period, based on the architecture of the Italian Renaissance and rural northern Italy. In the late 1850s houses that were being built in the Greek Revival style gradually began adding Italianate features and ornaments, and the highly detailed Italianate houses of the 1860s and 1870s came about.

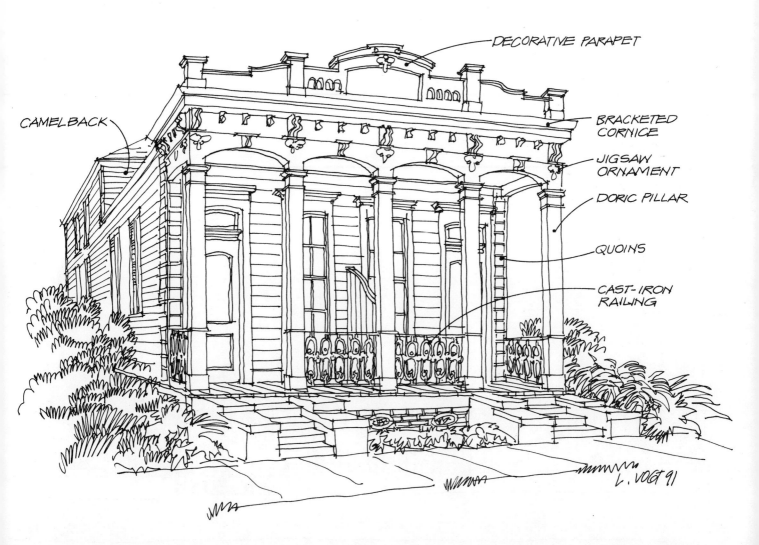

CAMELBACK

DECORATIVE PARAPET

BRACKETED CORNICE

JIGSAW ORNAMENT

DORIC PILLAR

QUOINS

CAST-IRON RAILING

L. VOGT 91

New Orleans felt the consequences of the Civil War, but its economy was not nearly as affected as most of the South's. Soon after the war ended in 1865, the city began to recover and construction, which had almost stopped during the war, began to increase. During the 1860s and 1870s development continued upriver along the streetcar line on St. Charles Avenue, slowly closing the gap between the urban area of New Orleans and the town of Carrollton, which had developed where St. Charles now meets Carrollton Avenue.

New Orleans had always been a crowded city by Southern standards, partly because of its tighter, European building traditions and partly because of the limited amount of dry, usable land. As the population continued to grow, land became more and more scarce. The space-saving shotgun house type, ideally suited for long, narrow lots, was a natural for these conditions. Thousands of shotgun houses, mostly two-bay singles and four-bay doubles, were constructed during this period.

Around 1900, classically inspired houses, painted all white, were again becoming popular, and the Victorian period was coming to an end. It had been a period that borrowed little from the past, a period that created its own tastes and standards — a period unlike any other in American history.

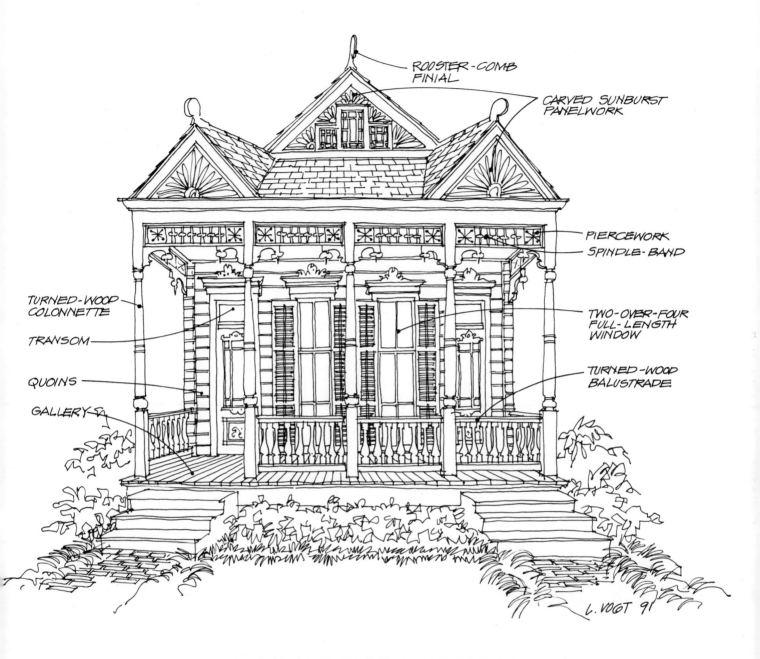

Labels on illustration:

ROOSTER-COMB FINIAL

CARVED SUNBURST PANELWORK

PIERCEWORK SPINDLE-BAND

TURNED-WOOD COLONNETTE

TRANSOM

TWO-OVER-FOUR FULL-LENGTH WINDOW

TURNED-WOOD BALUSTRADE

QUOINS

GALLERY

L. VOGT 91

EASTLAKE SHOTGUN DOUBLE

This house is an Eastlake style shotgun double, which means it is a house where two families live, one on each side. It is of a type and style that are very common in New Orleans. The Eastlake style gets its name from an English architect named Charles Locke Eastlake. Mr. Eastlake wrote a book about furniture design in 1868 which included drawings of furniture with all types of beautifully carved and cut woodwork. His book became very popular and soon American designers and builders began to use Eastlake's furniture woodwork designs on their houses.

BRACKET SHOTGUN SINGLE

This is a Bracket style house of the shotgun single type. These houses are very common in New Orleans. They can be identified by the large, fancy **brackets** that support the roof covering the front porch.

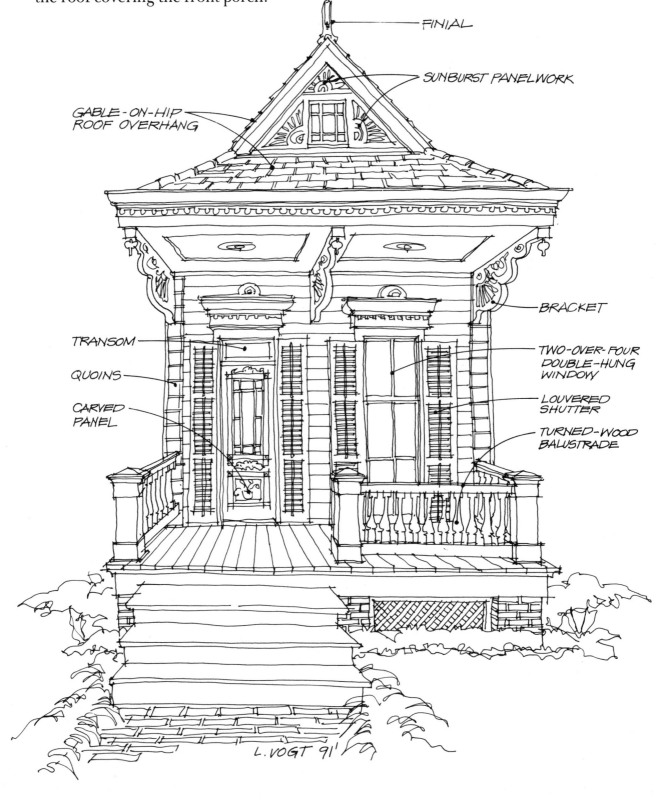

FINIAL

SUNBURST PANELWORK

GABLE-ON-HIP ROOF OVERHANG

BRACKET

TRANSOM

TWO-OVER-FOUR DOUBLE-HUNG WINDOW

QUOINS

LOUVERED SHUTTER

CARVED PANEL

TURNED-WOOD BALUSTRADE

L. VOGT 91'

QUEEN ANNE HOUSE

The Queen Anne style came from England and was introduced to Americans at the Philadelphia Exposition in 1876. The style is best identified by its irregular shape, and the combination of different roof types on one house. It is very ornamented, and always features a front porch — sometimes a very large one. Often different types of shingles or siding are used on Queen Anne houses, giving an interesting look to the outside.

This Queen Anne house is typical of many found in New Orleans. A large turret (tower) is located on one side, a common feature of Queen Anne houses.

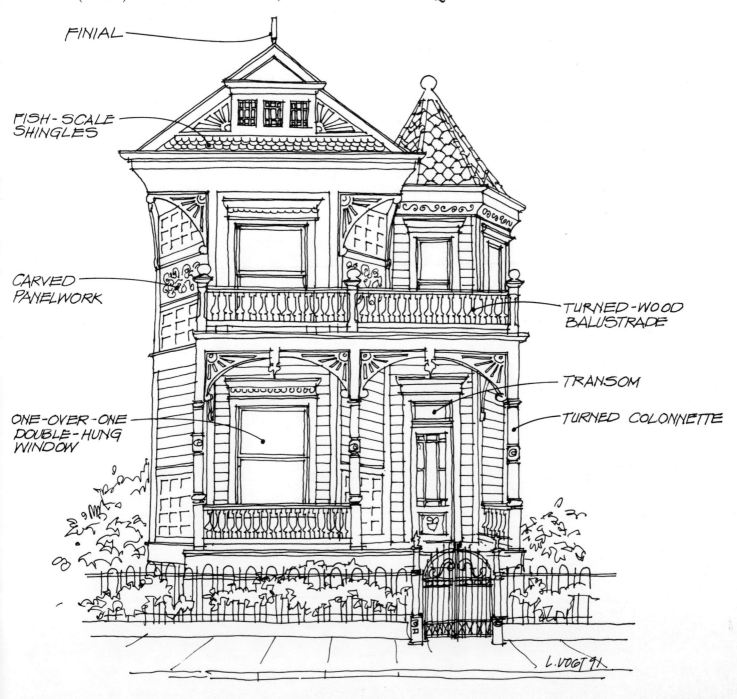

FINIAL

FISH-SCALE SHINGLES

CARVED PANELWORK

ONE-OVER-ONE DOUBLE-HUNG WINDOW

TURNED-WOOD BALUSTRADE

TRANSOM

TURNED COLONNETTE

L. VOGT 9X

THE EARLY TWENTIETH CENTURY
(1900-1940)

The twentieth century promised the American family a new way of life. A great expansion of industry provided jobs throughout the country, which meant that people had more money to spend. Automobiles, telephones, and movie theaters soon became very popular. In New Orleans, the port was busy, jazz music was growing, and the city was enjoying grand opera, theater, and vaudeville comedy acts, plays, and musicals.

As the population of the city increased, more land was needed to build on. Much of the land surrounding the developed area was swampland, and could not be built upon. Around 1900, a clever New Orleans engineer named A. Baldwin Wood, trying to solve the problem of draining the water from the land, invented the screw pump. It was a major technological breakthrough. The screw pump could move huge amounts of water very quickly, making possible a modern, efficient drainage system that made large areas of swampland suddenly dry enough for development.

Along with the new technology of drainage pumps, automobiles, and steel bridges, the twentieth century brought with it new architecture. The leaders again looked to the past for inspiration. The texture and complexity of the Victorian period changed to a general feeling of restraint and formality, which was shown in the Georgian Colonial Revival and Neoclassical Revival styles and in numerous other mixed styles.

Georgian Colonial Revival and Neoclassical Revival houses were most often painted all white, in sharp contrast to the many colors of the Victorian era. Elaborately carved turned wooden columns were replaced by the classical orders, and stained glass lost its popularity.Construction expanded in the 1920s, and two new styles came to New Orleans by way of California: the bungalow and Spanish Colonial Revival.

NEOCLASSICAL REVIVAL HOUSE

This Neoclassical ("neo" means new) house is typical of many in New Orleans. The style was popularized by the World's Fair in Chicago in 1893. One of the most striking features of the architecture of the fair was the all-white color scheme. After years of dark, heavy colors, people's eyes were immediately attracted to the all-white look of the "new" classical style, and the architectural American Renaissance was born. Neoclassical Revival houses began to appear in New Orleans in the late 1890s and continued to be built for thirty years or more. Porches and galleries are located on the front only. Huge **porticos** are a common feature of the style.

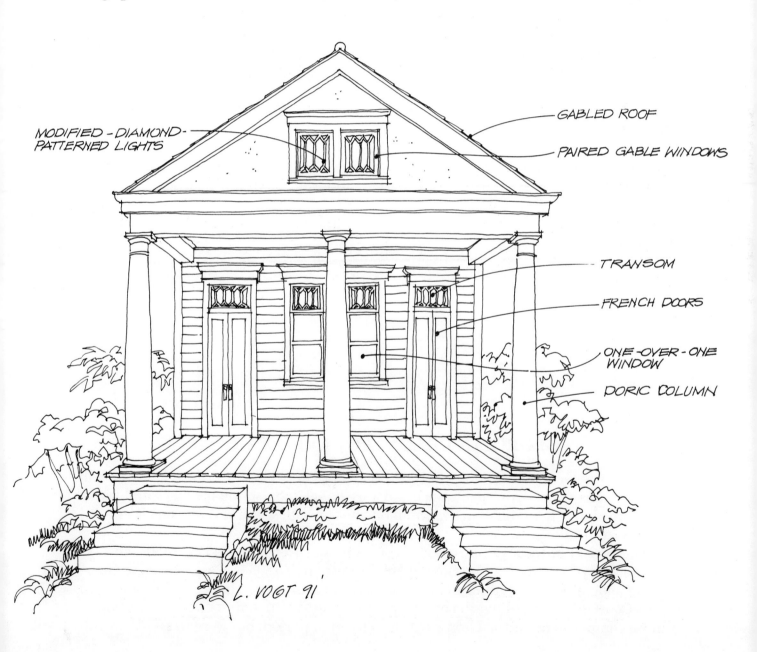

MODIFIED-DIAMOND-PATTERNED LIGHTS

GABLED ROOF

PAIRED GABLE WINDOWS

TRANSOM

FRENCH DOORS

ONE-OVER-ONE WINDOW

DORIC COLUMN

L. VOGT 91'

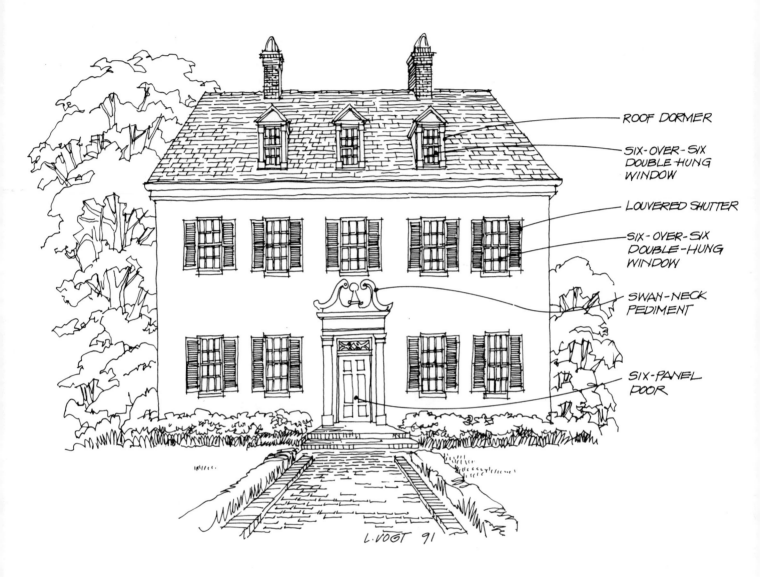

ROOF DORMER

SIX-OVER-SIX DOUBLE-HUNG WINDOW

LOUVERED SHUTTER

SIX-OVER-SIX DOUBLE-HUNG WINDOW

SWAN-NECK PEDIMENT

SIX-PANEL DOOR

L. VOGT 91

GEORGIAN COLONIAL REVIVAL HOUSE

Typical of Georgian Colonial Revival houses is this two-story, five-bay, center hall house. It has a very detailed entrance and a six-panel door, set slightly back and with a transom above. It is built of brick, and has windows with six panes over six others and **louvered** shutters.

The revival of the style started in the northeastern U.S. in the late 1880s, and received a lot of attention at the Columbian Exposition of 1893 in Chicago. Some Georgian Colonial Revival houses were copies of Georgian houses built on the American East Coast during the English colonial period (1700-1770). Others were based on the more complicated, unusual houses of the Victorian period, but were dressed up with colonial details.

BUNGALOW SHOTGUN DOUBLE

A very common sight in many neighborhoods of New Orleans, this wood-frame bungalow on brick piers has a front gallery with a gabled roof. The roof is supported by three paired, slightly tapered wooden posts, which are tripled at the corners and rest on **stucco pedestals**. The rafters are visible at the eaves of the roof, and the entrances are doors with numerous glass panes over wooden panels, and multipane **sidelights** and transoms.

The name "bungalow" comes from the Hindu word *bangla*, which means "a low house surrounded by porches." These houses were built in India as rest houses for foreign travelers, and served as the inspiration for the bungalows developed in the early 1900s in California. The popularity of the style rapidly spread as books of bungalow house plans circulated throughout America.

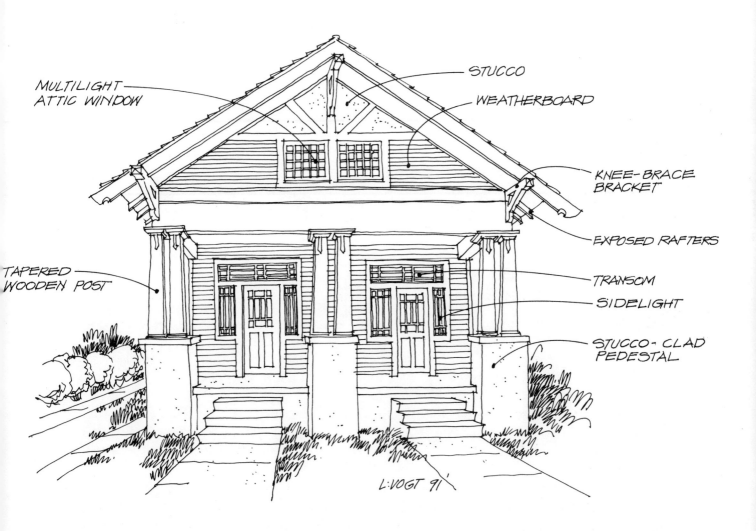

SPANISH COLONIAL REVIVAL

This Spanish Colonial Revival house has a low-**pitched** red **barrel-tile** roof, as well as a decorative parapet with iron grillwork and ball **finials** above a set-back or recessed entranceway. The entranceway features a door with many glass panes, a transom, and a decorative **cornice** above. It has smooth stucco walls, which are painted white.

Introduced at the 1915 Panama-California Exposition, the style is modeled after the missions and houses built by Spanish colonists in Florida and the Southwest, instead of those of Spanish colonial New Orleans.

BALL FINIAL

DECORATIVE PARAPET

BARREL TILE

TRANSOM

MULTILIGHT CASEMENT WINDOW

STUCCO

FRENCH DOORS

L. VOGT 91

GLOSSARY

ABAT-VENT — A roof extension that is almost flat; the roof material rests on iron supports which come out from the front of the house near the roof line.

ARCH — A curved structural opening.

ARCHITRAVE — The lowest part of an entablature.

ATTIC — All the space between the roof and ceilings of a building.

BALCONY — A platform or walking area that sticks out from an upper floor of a building and is surrounded by a railing.

BALUSTER — A generally slender post-like object that is used to support a handrail.

BALUSTRADE — A railing (such as a porch railing) made up of rails, balusters, and posts.

BARREL TILE — Clay roof tile named for the fact that it is shaped like a barrel cut in half from top to bottom.

BAYS — Repeated sections into which a building is divided, usually by columns.

BEVELED GLASS — Glass with beveled (cut on an angle) edges. Windows made of small pieces of beveled glass held together by lead strips were popular in the early twentieth century.

BRACKET — A support structure under the eaves of a roof, balcony, or other over-hang. Frequently used as decoration rather than for real structural support.

CANTILEVERED — A projection from a building that is not supported by pillars or columns. A gallery or balcony is cantilevered if there are no vertical supports hold-ing it up.

CAPITAL — The top part of a column.

CASEMENT WINDOW — A window that opens on hinges like a door; a common win-dow type in colonial New Orleans.

CAST IRON — Iron shaped by pouring it into a mold while melted. Used for railings, fences, etc.

CLASSICAL ARCHITECTURE — The architecture of Greece and Rome during the pre-Christian era.

COLONNETTE — A slender, turned, wooden column.

COLUMN — A vertical support which normally has a base, a round shaft, and a capital.

CORINTHIAN ORDER — The most highly detailed of the classical Greek orders. It can be identified by the unusual capitals of its columns, which are shaped like an upside-down bell covered with leaves.

CORNICE — The upper section of an entablature which sticks out slightly from the building, or the ornamental trim along the top edge of a building.

COURTYARD — An enclosed, open-air space next to a building.

CREOLE — A person born in the New World and descended from French and/or Spanish colonists. Also a style of architecture that was popular during the post-colonial period in New Orleans.

DENTILS — Closely spaced decorative blocks which look a little like teeth and are found in Greek Ionic and Corinthian cornices.

DORIC ORDER — The simplest of the classical Greek orders. It can be identified by columns with simple capitals and no bases.

DORMER — A small section of a building that usually has windows and its own roof covering and which sticks out from a house's wall or roof. When it is part of the roof it is called a roof dormer and when it is part of a wall it is called a wall dormer.

DOUBLE — A two-family house.

DOUBLE-HUNG WINDOW — A window type introduced to New Orleans in the early 1800s, consisting of two sashes that move up and down, usually with the aid of counterweights in the walls.

DOUBLE-PITCHED ROOF — A roof type common in the colonial era that has two different slopes or pitches.

EAVE — The overhang of a roof.

ENTABLATURE — In classical architecture, the long, horizontal structure that lies across the tops of all of the columns and supports the roof. The entablature is made up of the architrave, the frieze, and the cornice.

FACADE — The front wall of a building.

FINIAL — The decorative ornaments put on the tops of roof gables, turrets, railing posts, etc.

FIRE WALLS — Brick walls built on the ends of a building, or built between two buildings that are attached together and extended above the roofline of both buildings. Fire walls are intended to prevent fire from spreading from one building to another.

FRENCH DOORS — A pair of hinged doors, generally with glass lights (panes).

FRIEZE — The middle part of an entablature.

GABLE — The triangular upper part of a wall that is formed by a pitched roof.

GABLE-ON-HIP ROOF — The combination of a gable and a hipped roof.

GALLERY — Space that is open to the outside but is still under the main roof of a house. Compare with "Porch."

GREEK KEY SURROUND — A detail where the top of a door or window trim extends a little beyond the side trim, and the side trim flares out a little towards the bottom.

HIPPED ROOF — A roof with four equally sloped sides.

IONIC ORDER — An order of classical Greek architecture. It can be identified by the capitals of its columns, which look like rolled-up scrolls.

LIGHT — A glass pane in a window or door.

LOUVER — Louvers are the small, wooden blades in shutters. Sometimes they are fixed in place and cannot move, but generally they are movable so that they can be adjusted to let the desired amount of air and sunlight enter the room.

ORDER — An order in classical architecture is a specified way of designing and decorating the column, shaft, capital, and entablature. The three classical Greek orders are Doric, Ionic, and Corinthian.

ORNAMENTS — Elements or pieces added to a building for the purpose of decorating or adding beauty. Ornaments are not essential to the structure of a building. An example of ornaments is the elaborate woodwork added to Victorian houses.

PARAPET — A low wall, railing, or decorative projection along the edge of a roof.

PEDESTAL — A support base for a column.

PEDIMENT — A low-pitched gable in the classical manner; also used in miniature over doors or windows.

PIERCEWORK — Patterns created by carving openings of various shapes and sizes in wooden ornamental decorations.

PIERS — Square or rectangular supports for a house. Usually made of brick and sometimes covered with stucco.

PILLAR — A square or rectangular column.

PITCH — The angle or slope of a roof.

PLASTER — A mixture of lime, water, and sand that is soft when applied and hardens when dry. It is used for coating walls and ceilings.

PORCH — Outside space that is attached to a house, but has a separate roof. Compare with "Gallery."

PORTE COCHERE — A covered entrance for the passage of vehicles to the back of a building.

PORTICO — A covered, porch-like entrance to a building.

QUOINS — A stone, brick, or wood block used on the corners of buildings for decoration.

RAFTER — The top structural member of a sloped roof.

ROW HOUSES — Single-family houses attached to one another and built in rows.

SEGMENTAL ARCH — An arch design, usually the top of a window or door, which is in the shape of a portion of a circle.

SHED ROOF — A roof that is pitched or angled in only one direction.

SHINGLES — A wall or roof covering that is made up of small, overlapping pieces which are rectangular or patterned.

SHUTTER — A hinged cover, usually of wood, for a window or door.

SIDELIGHTS — Fixed, non-movable glass panes on either side of an entrance door.

SIDING — The material used to cover the side of a wood-frame building.

SINGLE — A one-family house.

SPINDLE — A turned decorative wooden element.

SPINDLE BAND — A row of spindles included as the uppermost decorative feature of a gallery or porch below the cornice. Also known as an open-work frieze.

STAINED GLASS — Colored glass.

STUCCO — Exterior plaster.

TURNED WOOD — Carved wooden elements such as spindles or balusters produced by being turned on a cutting machine called a lathe.

TRANSOM — A glass-filled opening over a door or window. Used for extra ventilation.

TRIM — The architectural finishing touches on a building or in a room. (The carved casings around windows and doors, for example.)

WEATHERBOARD — A long, narrow board, usually slightly thicker on the lower edge, that is used for siding. It runs horizontally and each board overlaps the one under it. Also known as "clapboard."

WOOD FRAME — Refers to a building whose structure is composed of boards held together with nails or pegs.

WROUGHT IRON — Iron worked into shape by manual effort. Used for balcony railings, fences, gates, lanterns, etc.